© 2010 Disney Enterprises, Inc.
Based on the book *The Hundred and One Dalmatians*
by Dodie Smith, published by The Viking Press.
Published by Hachette Partworks Ltd
ISBN: 978-1-906965-11-2
Date of Printing: November 2010
Printed in Singapore by Tien Wah Press

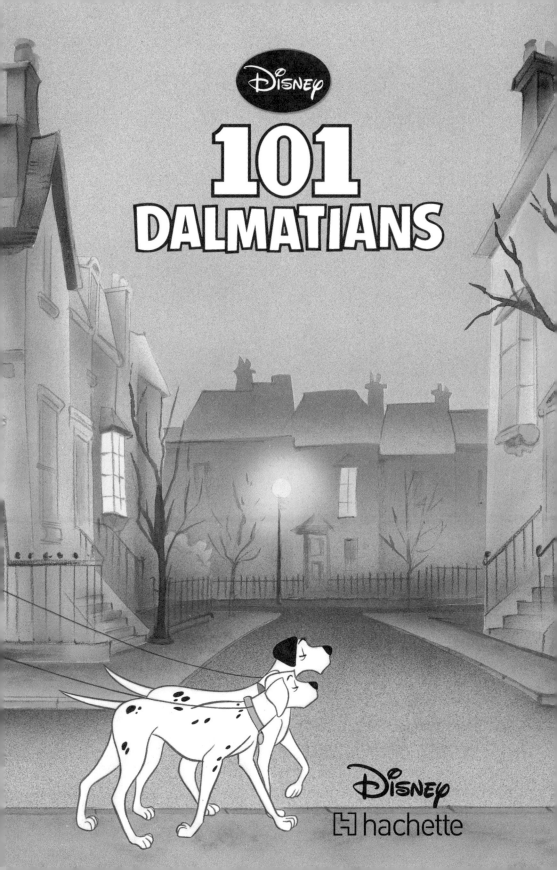

Our story begins in London, not so very long ago.
Two Dalmatians, Pongo and Perdita, lived in a nice,
comfortable house with Anita and Roger Radcliff, their
owners. Nanny looked after everyone.

One day, Pongo had some wonderful news. Perdita was going to have puppies! Everybody in the house was so happy and excited.

At last, the great day dawned.

"The puppies are coming!" shouted Nanny.

"How many?" asked Roger.

"Eight!" Nanny replied.

"Eleven!" chipped in Anita, from the other room.

"Thirteen! No, fourteen! Wait... fifteen!" Nanny added.

Fifteen puppies! Perdy
was delighted.
  "Pongo, you old rascal!"
exclaimed Roger.

The pups were adorable.
  "Their spots will appear in a little while,"
promised Nanny.

Suddenly, there
was a thunderous
sound. At the door
was Cruella De
Vil, Anita's old
schoolmate, in her
long fur cape. She
had come to check
on the puppies.
"I'll take them
all!" roared Cruella.

"They're not for sale,"
snapped Roger.
"You'll be sorry!" said
Cruella, slamming the
door behind her and
smashing the glass.
Pongo and Perdy
heaved a sigh of relief!

But Cruella didn't give up. She hired two
scoundrels, Jasper and Horace, to steal the puppies.

Meanwhile, the pups grew bigger and their fur became dotted with black spots.

The puppies loved watching television. Their favourite programme was all about the adventures of a very brave dog called Thunderbolt.

"Come on, Thunderbolt!" shouted Penny.

Once the show was over, Pongo sent the puppies off to bed.

"But we aren't sleepy!" complained Lucky.

As soon as the puppies were asleep, Pongo and Perdy went off to the park with Anita and Roger.

But the moment they left the house, Jasper and Horace tricked their way in!

Jasper shut poor Nanny in an upstairs room, while Horace bundled the puppies into a sack.

When Anita and Roger got back, Nanny told them what had happened. The police came and searched everywhere, but they found no trace of the puppies.

Pongo and Perdita were heartbroken.

Then Pongo had an idea. "What about the Twilight Bark, Perdy?" he said. "Every dog in town will hear it. If our puppies are still in London, someone will know."

Pongo began to bark in a special code. "Ruff, ruff, ruff! Fifteen Dalmatian pups stolen!"

The message passed
from dog to dog, until
it woke Tony the
bloodhound. He lived
on a farm out of town.

The Twilight Bark
was working well!

"Hmmm. A message from London," said Tony
to Lucy the goose.
   Tony passed the message on to the farmhouse,
waking up Captain the horse.

Captain told
Sergeant Tibbs,
the cat, to wake
the Colonel, an Old
English sheepdog.

The Colonel pricked up his ears, so he could hear
better. "Someone has stolen fifteen spotted poppies!" he
barked.

"Puppies, Colonel," corrected Sergeant Tibbs.

Captain remembered that he had heard barking
coming from the old De Vil manor.

"Nonsense!" said the Colonel. "No one has lived
there in years."

"But sir," protested Captain, "there's smoke
coming from the chimney!"

"I suppose we'd better check," muttered the
Colonel. Little by little, they crept towards the
gloomy old house.

Sergeant Tibbs sneaked inside. And what did he see? No fewer than ninety-nine Dalmatian puppies! But only fifteen were watching the television.

"Those must be the stolen pups," thought Tibbs, and he rushed back to raise the alarm.

The Colonel sent out a new message. It passed from dog to dog, all the way back to town. Pongo picked it up.

"The Great Dane has news!" he said. Pongo and Perdy rushed off to see the giant dog.

"The puppies have been spotted in the North," the Great Dane announced.

"We must go there, right now!" gasped Perdy.

When they reached the snowy countryside, they found Sergeant Tibbs and the Colonel waiting for them.

"No time to explain. Follow me!" barked the Colonel.
They let themselves into the old house. Of course, the
puppies were delighted to see them!

Pups were scampering everywhere. "There's ninety-
nine of us, dad!" said Lucky.

Pongo was puzzled. "What does Cruella want with so
many puppies?" he asked.

"She wants to make us into coats," replied Lucky.
Perdy was frightened. "She's a witch! What will we do?"
"We'll bring every puppy home with us," replied Pongo.
Sergeant Tibbs led the pups away. Jasper and Horace
didn't notice – they were busy watching television!

The dogs followed Sergeant Tibbs to the farmhouse. But they were not out of danger. As soon as Jasper and Horace realised that the puppies had escaped, they jumped into a van and began to follow the pawprints in the snow.

Captain was keeping watch. "Headlights ahead, Colonel!" he shouted.

"It's those two villains, Jasper and Horace," exclaimed Sergeant Tibbs.

Pongo frowned. "We'd better run for it!"

The Dalmatians scrambled out of the back door. But Horace and Jasper were greeted by a fierce kick from Captain that sent them hurtling through the main gate!

Pongo and Perdy were leading the pups to safety.
But suddenly, Pongo heard the sound of a car engine.
All the Dalmatians hid under a bridge. Luckily,
Jasper and Horace failed to spot them!

Pongo decided that they should start walking on the frozen river, so they wouldn't leave pawprints for Jasper and Horace to follow. But it was very cold and a blizzard was starting.

The puppies were tired and hungry. "My tail is frozen. My nose and ears are frozen. And so are my paws!" complained Lucky.

Just then, Pongo heard a friendly voice. A collie appeared. "You can find shelter on the other side of the road," he said.

The collie took them to a barn, where kindly cows gave the hungry pups some milk. It wasn't long before every one of the ninety-nine puppies was fast asleep in the hay.

Pongo and Perdy thanked the cows and the collie and they too fell asleep, exhausted.

The next day, the Dalmatians set off again. In the next village, a black Labrador was waiting to help them. But Pongo knew only too well that Cruella wouldn't give up the search.

He tried his best to hide their tracks, brushing
the pawprints away with a branch.

But Cruella spotted them anyway! "These
prints are leading straight towards the village,"
she snarled at Jasper and Horace.

When the dogs reached the
village, the Labrador took them
straight to an old, empty building.
"See that van?" he asked. "It's
going to London, and there's room
for you all inside!"

But then they saw Cruella's car pull up. She was furious with Jasper and Horace. The villains began to comb the streets, looking for the puppies.

"How will we get to the van?" despaired Perdy.

At that moment, Lucky piped up: "Dad! Spot pushed me into the fireplace!" Poor Lucky was covered in soot.

"He pushed me first!" argued Spot, who was also completely sooty and black.

Pongo looked very thoughtful...

Then Pongo rolled in the soot and said, "Look. I've turned into a Labrador! Let's all cover ourselves in soot and no one will know we're Dalmatians!"

"That'll fool the old witch!" giggled the pups.

The van was ready to leave.
"No time to lose," said their pal, the real Labrador.
One by one, the puppies climbed aboard.

As soon as they made it onto the van, some water
dripped down from the roof on to a few of the pups,
washing away the soot!

Now, Cruella could recognise the dogs. "There they are!" she shouted. Luckily, the van sped off in the nick of time.

"Get them! Follow that van!" Cruella screeched.

But Cruella was driving much too fast on the slippery road. Her car crashed into the van driven by Jasper and Horace! The three of them ended up in a ditch, covered in snow. The dogs zoomed ahead in their van.

Back in London, Anita and Nanny were putting the decorations on the Christmas tree. Roger was too upset to help.

"Sometimes, at night, I think I can hear them barking," he said sadly. "Then I realise I'm dreaming."

Then Nanny
heard a noise.
She ran to
open the door.
A big black dog
bounded into
Roger's arms,
covering him in
kisses and soot!

"It's a family of
Labradors!" said
Roger.

Nanny wiped
the puppies down.
"No," she gasped,
"this is soot. Look,
it's Lucky!"

The house was
full of dogs: no
fewer than one
hundred and one
Dalmatians!

"What will we do now?" asked Anita.

"We'll buy a bigger house, in the country," Roger declared, "and we'll raise them all!" After their thrilling adventures, Roger, Anita and all the Dalmatians had a truly magical Christmas!